MARY ANN

Betsy James

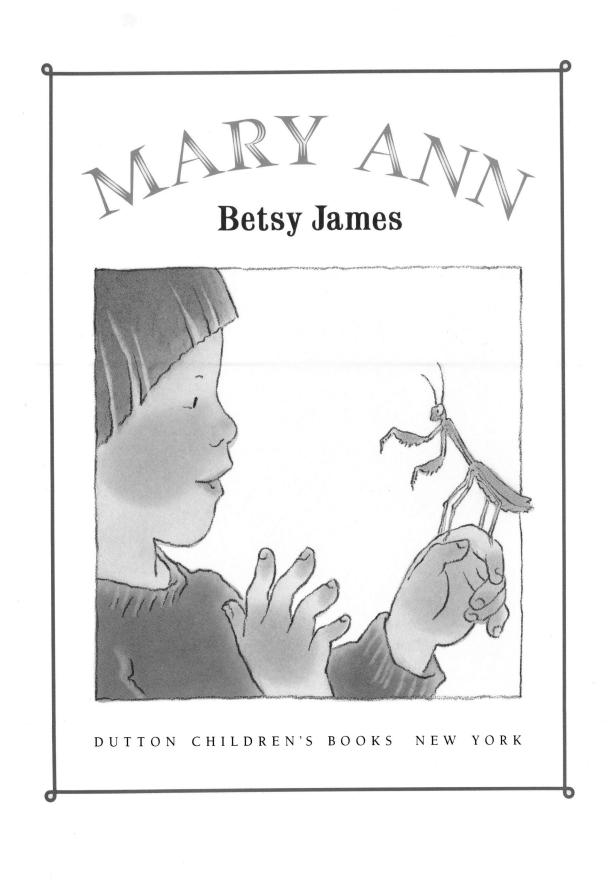

DUTTON CHILDREN'S BOOKS NEW YORK

Library of Congress Cataloging-in-Publication Data

James, Betsy.

Mary Ann/ by Betsy James.—1st ed.   p.   cm.

Summary: After her best friend, Mary Ann, moves away,

Amy finds a praying mantis and names her Mary Ann.

ISBN 0-525-45077-7   [1. Praying mantis–Fiction.

2. Friendship–Fiction.]   I. Title.   PZ7.J15357Mar

1994   [E]—dc20   93-13364   CIP   AC

Published in the United States 1994

by Dutton Children's Books,

a division of Penguin Books USA Inc.

375 Hudson Street, New York, New York 10014

Designed by Adrian Leichter

Printed in Hong Kong

First Edition

10 9 8 7 6 5 4 3 2 1

For Heidi and Hilary,

whose dad remembers Mary Ann

Mary Ann lived next door. She was my best friend. Our birthdays were on the same day, and green was our favorite color.

We made banana-marshmallow pancakes and built a
secret clubhouse under the juniper bush in my backyard.
But Mary Ann moved away.

Mary Ann didn't come over to make pancakes anymore.

She didn't play in my bedroom

or under the juniper bush.

"It's not fair!" I said. "She was my best friend!"

Daddy said, "Sometimes best friends move away, and we feel sad. That's how it is."

"I wish there were hundreds and hundreds of Mary Anns," I said. "Then if one moved away, it wouldn't matter."

Our clubhouse was empty. But a strange green bug was climbing a juniper twig. "Daddy," I said, "what's this?"

"Good for you, Amy," Daddy said. "You've found a praying mantis. Would you like to keep her? Hold out your hand, and she'll step onto it."

I said, "I'll name her Mary Ann!"

In the kitchen I had a terrarium made out of an old fish tank with a piece of screen for a lid. It made a good house for Mary Ann. When I put her inside, she climbed a tall fern and waved her arms at me.

Every day I took off the screen and sprinkled a little water on the ferns, like raindrops, for her to drink.

Sometimes I held out my hand. Then she would walk up my arm with her tickly feet and drink water from a spoon.

We had to feed Mary Ann every day. She ate a lot! We caught grasshoppers and butterflies for her. Under rocks we found crickets and ants.

I put the bugs in the terrarium, and Mary Ann munched them like sandwiches.

Sometimes she liked a crumb of raw hamburger. When she was finished, she cleaned her face with her front legs, the way our cat washed with his paws.

Every day she got fatter. Then, when summer was over, she pushed a ball of foam out of her tail, onto a fern stem.

"Her eggs are inside the ball," said Mama. "Hundreds and hundreds of eggs."

But after she laid her eggs, Mary Ann walked slower and
slower. She wouldn't eat crickets. She wouldn't drink from
her spoon. And one morning, when I came to breakfast,
Mary Ann was dead.

I cried.

We put Mary Ann in an empty box and buried her under the juniper bush.

"It's not fair!" I said. "She was my best friend!"

"I know it makes you sad," said Mama. "We talked about how a praying mantis dies after she lays her eggs. That's how it is. But we'll keep the screen on the terrarium, and we'll wait and watch for Mary Ann's eggs to hatch."

I waited.

And waited.

I waited for weeks and weeks—all winter—

until it was almost spring.

Mary Ann's eggs didn't hatch.

"I don't have any best friend," I said to Daddy.

"Sometimes friends move away," said Daddy. "But we can still visit them!"

So we packed up the car. We locked the house.

We drove and drove until we came to another town,

to another house,

and there on the doorstep was Mary Ann!

I played with Mary Ann in the kitchen

and in the backyard.

We built a new clubhouse in her bunk bed

and made banana-marshmallow pancakes in the morning.

Then it was time to say good-bye.

"We'll come visit again soon!" we promised.

We drove back home, we unlocked the door,

and turned on the light.

"The eggs!" yelled Daddy. "They hatched!"

Mama yelled, "Oh no—the screen was off the terrarium!"

But I yelled, "Look at all the Mary Anns!"

There were Mary Anns in the teacups,

on the toaster,

and the telephone.

There were Mary Anns under the soap,

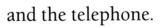

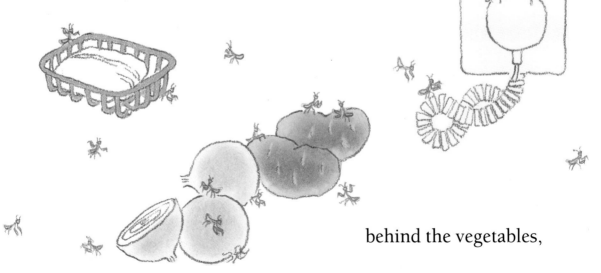

behind the vegetables,

and in the honey.

There were Mary Anns on the butter

and all over the geraniums.

There were Mary Anns *everywhere*.

I had hundreds and hundreds of Mary Anns!

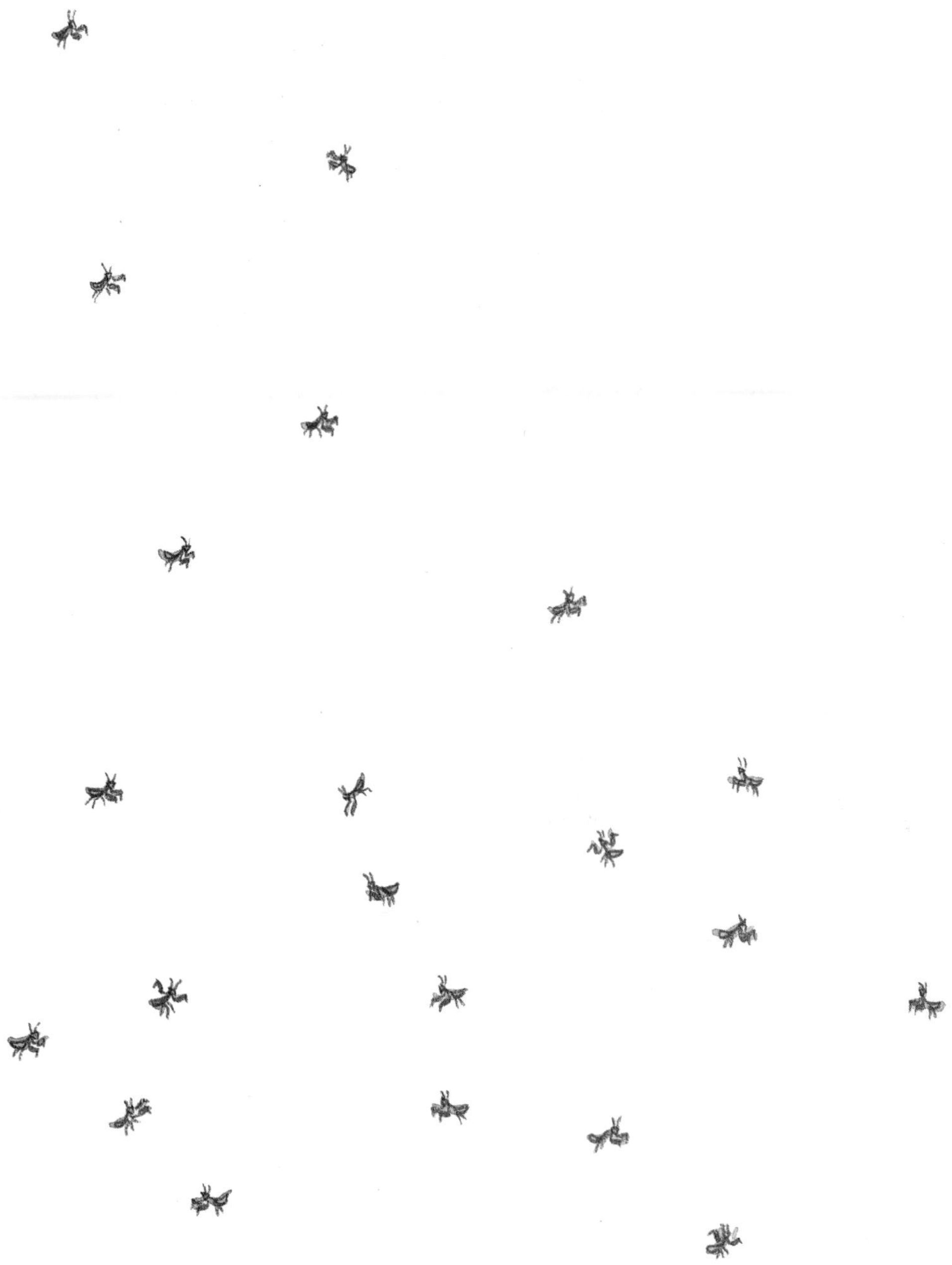

Praying mantises are found all over the world. They are fascinating and useful insects with triangular, movable heads and with forelegs that are often held in a prayerlike position, which gives them their name.

You might find a praying mantis among flowers in a garden or on the leaves of a bush. In spring, mantises may be hardly bigger than a mosquito, while in late summer they may grow to as long as three inches.

In most states, you may keep a mantis in your house. Check with your local reference librarian or natural history museum, however, because some states have laws against capturing mantises.

If you find a mantis and would like to keep it, give it a home with lots of air and light and plants—Amy's big terrarium was perfect. Don't forget to place a dish of drinking water in the terrarium and keep it full and clean.

A mantis will eat almost any kind of little animal that crawls or flies or squirms, such as crickets, grasshoppers, or worms. It will also eat raw chicken or hamburger (but only in tiny bits). Feed your mantis every day.

Never try to pick up a mantis, because you might frighten or hurt it. Instead, *very slowly* offer it the back of your hand, and it will climb on. Once it feels comfortable, it will walk up your arm and eat from your fingers or drink water from a spoon.

Late summer is the best time to hunt for a female mantis who will lay eggs. A female who is ready to lay her eggs will have a plump abdomen. Be sure she has a strong twig in her mantis house on which to build her egg case. Like Mary Ann, she will die after she lays her eggs.

Important: *Do not* keep the mantis egg case indoors, as Amy did. The eggs need to stay at the naturally cold temperature of the outdoors or they will hatch too early in the spring. Leave the eggs in the mantis house and put it outside. Be sure the house's lid is on tight because 300 to 500 babies hatch out of every egg case!

The time of hatching will vary, depending on where you live. When you see tiny, waving legs and feelers on the surface of the egg case, carry the house to a place where there are plants and insects. Then take the lid off. The babies must start hunting for food right away; they're hungry, and if they can't find insects to eat, they will eat each other!

Mantises eat garden pests such as grasshoppers, so in the springtime some gardening stores and catalogs sell egg cases, ready to hatch. If you can't find a Mary Ann, you may be able to buy an egg case—it's a good way to make sure you'll have praying mantises in your garden all summer.